Malaya the Panada

By David G Evans

One day there lived a panda named Malaya, she had 1 brother Ju-long.

Her parents Li Jun and Da Xia are travelers who have been all around chia kingdom and other places far, far away.

They always bring back gifts for their daughter.

But the gifts have to be put together before they can be put on display.

Malaya enjoys pruning the families bonsai tree, and making things from wood, rope, and paper.

Her brother is very clumsy and sometimes ruins her projects, but he's forgiven.

One afternoon her brother, bumped into her rubber band ball, which was taller than a man.

It went rolling down the hill, then into the street.

The pandas were running for their lives, the dragon patrol saw the ball and went after it.

Eventually they were able to stop it, with the help of a samurai.

He sliced the ball in half, this was disheartening for her and she cried.

Later that day, after praying to the ruler of the kingdom.

Malaya was joined by her mother, while her father was working at the bamboo factory.

Today I’ll teach you how to make bamboo candy, you know that I don’t like sweet things.

“Where’s your brother?”

“He’s out in the yard tending to the plum tree.”

“Did you tell him to do that?”

"No."

Your father taught him how to make plum candy treats.

Now he's obsessed with eating the candy.

"Are we going to the arena tomorrow to see the samurai games?"

“Yes,” we are.

“What are you cooking?”

“An Herbal remedy for your dad.”

He complained this morning, of having stomach pain.

Her mother looked out the window

She saw her brother climbing up on the branches.

“Does your brother always climb up on the branches?”

“Yes.”

Suddenly a paper airplane, came flying in through the open window.

Malaya went over to the window and picked up the paper airplane, and quickly unraveled it.

In bold lettering it said from the dragon.

She took it over to her mother.

“Where did you get this?”

“By the window.”

It's just the neighbor's kid, being silly.

Maybe we should invite the neighbor's kid over here.

He can do origami with us, that would be nice.

Tonight, for dinner we're having beef soup with vegetables.

I've always enjoyed eating that.

“Where are you going mom?”

“To check on your brother.”

After she came back in her father arrived home, he was all sweated and bothered.

You both won't believe what I went through.

On my way home, I saw that the forest was on fire.

One of the flames had gone across the road, so I had to go a different way.

Malaya gave her dad a bear hug, you're the most wonderful dad.

Thanks, that took my stress away.

"Who made that origami bird on the windowsill?"

“I did” said Malaya.

You could make that into a business, it would be very successful.

I'm surprised that your brother, isn't in here to greet me.

Their father went over to the window and saw her brother tumbling around in the yard.

He's being very disgraceful; he should be respecting me his elder.

He called his name, and he came running in the door.

“Where have your manners gone?”

“I was just having a good time.”

Then her brother bowed to their father.

You must always respect your elders authority no matter what.

Now you can go to your room, you just showed me that you can do the right thing.

If he doesn't learn, he’ll be going down a treacherous trail to despair.

Some time passed, and now it was dinner time.

They were all sitting around the kitchen table and began to eat.

I made some extra potatoes if anyone wants them.

Her brother spoke out I would please.

Their mother passed him the potato, thanks.

After dinner was over, they had a long conversation with each other.

A few hours passed and now it was bedtime.

Their daughter and her brother fell asleep before their parents did.

The next day, everyone came out to have their breakfast together.

Malaya yawned, and her brother giggled at her.

You're lucky that your father didn't hear you laughing like that, I know.

Her brother grabbed a piece of melon, and a plum.

Remember you can only take things that you're going to eat, we're going through a scarcity of food.

Their father took the plum from her brother and cut it in half.

Her brother had a dumbfounded look on his face, you and I are going to share this now.

“Whose going to help your mother today with the gardening?”

“Malaya quickly spoke up before, her brother had a chance.”

Next time your brother is going to be volunteering.

We must master the art of growing things in a garden, to make the ancients happy.

After another discussion, they were all packed up in the car, and on the way to the arena.

The only one with a smile on their face was Malaya.

Her brother was taking in the sites.

Today there was a lot of traffic.

Her brother pointed to something out the window.

You better not, let your father see you doing that.

Their mother took a quick glance back at them and continued the conversation with their father.

Sometime later they entered the arena.

Before they knew it, the show was started.

2 samurai's came out into the middle of the arena and bowed down to the audience.

They got the fruit chucker ready, and it fired a watermelon at them.

Hi yah, and the watermelon was sliced in half.

Look someone in the audience is booing them.

He just threw a water balloon at them.

The samurai shouted out you disrespectful man.

The gates behind them opened up, and an elephant walked in.

I wonder what he's doing here.

It's just a new act in the show.

The elephant picked up some oranges and began juggling them.

After that act was over, then for the next act the elephant breezed fire.

They looked over at their father and his eyes were glued to the elephant.

It doesn't take much to amuse our father.

Just let him enjoy the show.

The samurai's continued swinging their swords, effortlessly cutting up the fruit.

Before they knew it, the show was over.

Luckily they got out of there, before the crowds of panadas filled the streets.

They got back to the car and took off down the road.

The regular road was closed.

They followed the detour home.

Once they got back, their father noticed that there were several pray mantis in their garden.

When he was about to turn to walk away, they flew up into the air and landed on his back.

Malaya knew what to do.

She quickly went over and took them off his back and set them down on the fence.

Her brother just looked on.

I don't have any interest in playing with bugs and went back in the house.

After that, their father retreated back into the house.

Malaya and her mother worked on the garden, for the rest of the afternoon.

www.ingramcontent.com/pod-product-compliance
Lightning Source LLC
LaVergne TN
LVHW020543160826
845677LV00015B/4182
* 9 7 9 8 8 4 8 3 6 4 7 9 8 *